TIGERELLA

TIGERELLA
~ KIT WRIGHT ~

PICTURES BY
PETER BAILEY

SCHOLASTIC
HARDCOVER

SCHOLASTIC INC.
New York

Library of Congress Cataloging-in-Publication Data

Wright, Kit.
Tigerella / by Kit Wright; illustrated by Peter Bailey.
p.   cm.
Summary: By day, Ella is a well-behaved girl, but at night, she becomes
Tigerella and frolics among the stars.
ISBN 0-590-48171-1
[1. Behavior — Fiction. 2. Tigers — Fiction. 3. Stars — Fiction.
4. Stories in rhyme.] I. Bailey, Peter, ill. II. Title.
PZ8.3 W936Ti 1994
[E] — dc20   93-34218
                              CIP
                              AC

12 11 10 9 8 7 6 5 4 3 2 1   4 5 6 7 8 9/9

Printed in the U.S.A.   37

The illustrator used pen and ink, colored ink, and watercolors
for the paintings in this book.

ELLA

Ella was nice at the barbecue.
Everything Ella did
Was right.

She passed around the sausages
And even gave
The dog a bite.

She didn't tease the old tomcat
Or stamp on old Mr Rathbone's hat.
She never, ever did things like that

As *some*
Would have thought
She might.

No,

Ella was *fine* at the barbecue.
Ella behaved
Just right!

Good as gold and nice as pie,
She sweetly kissed each guest good-bye.
And they all said, "Ella, it's been a pleasure!
Ella, *aren't* you a little treasure!
We're just so sorry we have to go!"

you little treasure!

It's been a pleasure!

But
little
did
they
know...

They didn't know at all
That at the midnight stroke
Ella stirred in her bed
And a *changed* Ella woke

With a furry kind of growl
And hide of yellow and black
And whiskers and golden eyes
And a TAIL at the end of her back!

Softly she crept down the midnight stairs,
In the breathing dark her eyes shone bright,
And she poured herself from the open window
Onto the lawn in the mad moonlight.

TIGERELLA she was!
TIGERELLA her name!
A giant cat of the jungle
By moonlight she became!

Rippling over the silver grass
(She left no mark, she made no sound),
On she moved with flowing shoulders,
Wild One on the midnight ground.

Easily as her shadow
She glided over the wall.
She raised her head in the cornfield,
Seeing, scenting all...

And then she was gathering pace through the whispering hay fields,
Running, racing, the beat of her heart in tune
With the earth and the night and the creatures ~ until she coiled
And LEAPT and bit a piece from the rolling moon!

She tossed the stars about!
Tigerella at play!

How she bumped them,
How she battered them,

How she skittered them,
How she scattered them

Up and down
The Milky Way!

And soon through the bright star-clusters
She was traveling on;
By glittering constellations,
She sailed
        at the side
                of the Swan ...

Over the great calm lake of space ...

Until she soared and, face to face
And paw to paw, she found the Bear
And they jumbled and tumbled everywhere,
They tussled and hustled, wrestled and nestled,
Two beasts playing together there!

But Mighty Orion the Hunter
Gazed at the stars below.

Mighty Orion the Hunter
Raised his shimmering bow.

He sent an arrow whizzing
Down like a silver streak

Through the billion stars of the heavens
And grazed Tigerella's cheek!

So Tigerella turned
And raced in its track.

She caught it and she wheeled
And hurled that arrow back!

And then they were diving down through the huge unknown.
Wild star-cities they touched and they tumbled beyond,
As they fell through the dark of the night until they landed
On tingling paws
By Ella's
Garden
Pond!

They lapped the water. They licked each other's faces.
"See you again," they said. "So long. Take care."

Then Tigerella poured herself through the window,
And up to his home in the heavens soared the Bear ...

Ella was nice and polite at breakfast,
Ella sat quietly
At her place.

Her mother said, "Ella,
Did you sleep all right, dear?
What's that scratch there
On your face?"

Ella said, "Naughty old tomcat did it!"

"Did he? The wicked old
So-and-so!"

"Yes," said Ella, "Yes, he did!"

And
    little
        did
            they
                know!

DATE DUE

15 pm	MAR 2 9 '99	14	APR 2 5 2000
2	APR 2 7 '99	6	NOV 0 6 2000
9	JAN 1 8 2000	2	NOV 1 4 2000
16 pm	JAN 2 6 2000	12	NOV 2 8 2000
3	FEB 0 8 2000	10	DEC 1 5 2000
14	FEB 0 8 2000	18 pm	NOV 1 4 2001
5	FEB 1 5 2000	0	JAN 1 1 2001
21	MAR 2 8 2000	15	JAN 2 2 2002
4	APR 1 0 2000	7	JAN 2 9 2002

E   98152
Wri

Wright, Kit
  Tigerella

                    $14.95